after many years, a herc

returns.

the man of steel

is back...

SUPERMAN

R E T U R N S

THE OFFICIAL MOVIE GUIDE

Images courtesy of **Warner Bros. Pictures**   •   *Design by* **John J. Hill**   •   *Screenplay by* **Michael Dougherty & Dan Harris**
Story by **Bryan Singer & Michael Dougherty & Dan Harris**   •   *Superman created by* **Jerry Siegel and Joe Shuster**

*intro*duction

Т his torch is kind of heavy.

Before being handed to me, it was passed from one talented artist to another— from comic book illustrators, to animators, to musicians, to writers, and other filmmakers— continuing a tradition that was started by two kids from Ohio back in 1938. The torch has evolved quite a bit, maybe even been scratched a few times, but the flame has never gone out. I've been carrying it for almost two years now, doing my best to make sure it always burns bright and is handled with the utmost care.

But I didn't carry it alone.

From those who came before me, to the hundreds of individuals who helped me make this film a reality, keeping the Superman torch lit was a monumental task made possible only by teamwork. Everyone involved brought their own unique skill, and applied it with the same passion that their predecessors did over the character's 68-year history.

Eventually it will be passed to someone else, and like me, they'll quickly realize how heavy it is. But also like myself, they'll have the support and strength of not just the artists around them, but all those who came before.

- Bryan Singer

part 1: *the story*

continues

superman:
from comics to screen

Superman is the most famous super hero of all time, and one of the most potent and enduring cultural icons ever created. Even those who don't know anything about super-heroics can readily rattle off a laundry list of Superman's powers and abilities: Faster than a speeding bullet. More powerful than a locomotive. Bulletproof. Able to fly, see through walls, and fire heat beams from his eyes.

As Kal-El, the infant son of scientist Jor-El and his wife Lara, Superman escaped his doomed birthworld of Krypton before its destruction and landed in Smallville, Kansas. There, Jonathan and Martha Kent raised him as their adopted son Clark, grounding him in the principles of honesty and fair play as he gradually discovered that his powers could help humanity. As an adult, Clark moved to Metropolis and assumed a dual identity, working as a mild-mannered newspaper reporter for the *Daily Planet*, and soaring into action as the red, blue, and yellow-clad Superman to guard his city against menaces. Mad genius Lex Luthor is his perennial foe, while Lois Lane — his coworker at the *Daily Planet* — is the love of his life.

Created by Jerry Siegel and Joe Shuster, two science fiction pulp fans from Cleveland, Ohio, Superman was an immediate sensation following his debut in June 1938's *Action Comics #1*. As the character's popularity grew, Superman stories appeared in newspaper strips, radio serials, and theatrical cartoons. Kirk Alyn played the Man of Steel in movie serials during the 1940s, to be succeeded by George Reeves in television's *The Adventures of Superman* a decade later. Superman's small screen adventures are still going strong today with *Smallville*, a TV series that chronicles the young adult years of Clark Kent.

Many would say that the definitive telling of Superman's story came in 1978, with director Richard Donner's *Superman: The Movie*, which starred Christopher Reeve in the title role, and featured Gene Hackman as Lex Luthor and Marlon Brando as Jor-El. The film, which spawned three sequels, has attracted a legion of fans, including *Superman Returns* director Bryan Singer and screenwriters Michael Dougherty and Dan Harris. The three held such respect for the original that they conceived of *Superman Returns* as an unofficial sequel to the themes and situations of Donner's film.

Superman Returns marks Superman's return to movie screens after nearly two decades. At the start of the film, the Man of Steel reaches the planet of his birth, only to discover that Krypton is a cold graveyard. He comes back to his childhood home in Smallville, Kansas, then journeys to Metropolis, until it becomes painfully clear that the people he knew have not spent the last five years in stasis. Martha Kent is considering selling the farm and moving to Montana. Lois Lane is raising her five-year-old son with her new fiancēe. It appears that there may be some truth to Lois Lane's Pulitzer Prize-winning *Daily Planet* article, "Why the World Doesn't Need Superman." As *Superman Returns* unfolds, the Man of Steel struggles to find his place in the universe.

Of course, Lex Luthor is eager to spoil Superman's identity quest. The world's greatest criminal mind once again has grand designs on real estate, and his plan to raise the continent of New Krypton in the middle of the Atlantic imperils the entire world. Faced with his greatest challenge, Superman must harness his courage, his spirit, and all his Kryptonian powers to reclaim his role as humanity's protector.

*The cover of **Superman #1** from July 1939 presents an iconic image of the Man of Steel reproduced many times over the decades.*

Bryan Singer is the director of *Superman Returns*, tackling what might be his dream project. The film marks his sixth directorial release and his biggest project to date, both in budget and audience expectations.

Singer is no stranger to super heroes, having proved that the genre can support complex characters and mature themes with his directorial work on *X-Men* and *X2: X-Men United*. Superman has long occupied a place in Singer's imagination, in incarnations from the George Reeves television series to Richard Donner's *Superman: The Movie*.

With this degree of super-heroic material knocking around in his head, Singer felt the time was right to deal with the hero universally acknowledged as the original and best, and to mark the character's return with a story that would pay homage to what had gone before.

"It was always my intention to acknowledge the 1978 Donner film as a classic," says Singer. "Instead of attempting to retell it, I chose to place it in a kind of 'vague history' and begin from there." Since most moviegoers would already be familiar with Christopher Reeve's Superman and the origin story laid out in *Superman: The Movie*, Singer didn't need to retread the same ground. *Superman Returns* marks both Superman's return to Metropolis and his real-world return to the movie multiplex. "I always wanted it to be a return story," says Singer. "At first I didn't know where he would be returning from, but I wanted the character to have already existed, [and] to have had some kind of interaction with Lois Lane and Lex Luthor."

Placing *Superman Returns* into the tacit chronology of *Superman: The Movie* allowed Singer to make visual and thematic references to the 1978 film. Certain artifacts, such as the Fortress of Solitude, made the journey to *Superman Returns* virtually unchanged from their original source. By contrast, Singer chose to ignore the New York City footage used to simulate Metropolis in *Superman: The Movie*, instead reinventing Metropolis as a lively art-deco urban center in a nod to Superman's 1930s beginnings.

"Superman has to seem as though he's stepped out of the comic books," says Singer, "and also out of our collective memories. The character comes from the comic books, the radio serials, the George Reeves television program, and of course, the Richard Donner film. So I combined visual styles to create that feel, then brought to it a more modern story."

The maturity of the storyline adds a new level of complexity. When Superman comes back to Earth and discovers that Lois has found someone else, it's a conflict that he can't fight with his fists. "Superman is so incredibly impervious and powerful," says Singer, "that the only way you can hurt him, besides kryptonite, is at an emotional level. By giving Lois Lane a child, that's probably the most radical departure that we've taken. The world has moved on, Lois Lane has moved on, there's a fiancée involved, a child... there's all these very 'human' obstacles for the Man of Steel.

Singer views the Krypton-born Superman as the "ultimate immigrant." The outsider coming to terms with his role is the ultimate theme of *Superman Returns*. "Superman comes in as a vulnerable figure, trying to find his place in the world," says Singer. "I think by the end of the film he does. That's the journey of this movie: Superman reclaiming his place on the planet Earth."

director bryan singer

screenwriters michael dougherty and dan harris

Screenwriting partners Michael Dougherty and Dan Harris have enjoyed a rewarding relationship with Bryan Singer, having penned the script for the director's previous super hero film, *X-Men 2: X-Men United*. The experiences helped arm them for a daunting challenge: telling the story of the greatest super hero of them all.

Fortunately, Dougherty did most of his homework as a kid. "I was a geek," he confesses. "Growing up surrounded by piles of comic books and watching cartoons, [which] actually became research for a future career." Both writers had an understanding of the seven decades of accumulated Superman history, and counted themselves among the fans of 1978's *Superman: The Movie*. Although they wanted to create an entirely new Superman experience, they knew they weren't going get there by retooling the main character as "edgy" or dark. "[Superman] is a rock, unchanging over the course of his time in the American lexicon," says Harris. "The question is not how Superman is different this time around, it's how Superman is able to deal with the world being different from how he last remembered it."

It wouldn't be a Superman movie without certain iconic beats, such as Clark ripping open his shirt to reveal the costume beneath. "We tried to be really creative about how they were used," says Dougherty. We're trying to have fun with [Superman] catchphrases without being too obvious with them."

Another "must-have" moment is the image of bullets ricocheting off Superman's chest. A bank robbery scene was part of the original treatment, but later expanded in the screenplay to encompass something audiences had never seen before. "What is the most vulnerable place on the body, a place where no Superman incarnation has gone after?" Harris asks. "Basically, Bryan wanted Superman to get shot in the eye, to proudly and fully show how all-encompassing his invulnerability is."

Dougherty likens the script to a candy bar, describing such "It's a plane!" moments as the sprinkles, which sit atop the chewy center of the film — that is, a compelling story and meaningful theme. "It would be easy to say, we can have Superman go up against this villain, and that will be the core of the film," he says. "But what if he came home after five years and found out that the woman he loved has moved on with her life? [That] she had a kid and is about to marry someone else? For us, that was much more challenging, since it wasn't something he could use his powers against."

After a vacation in Hawaii where the idea for the film was hatched, Singer, Dougherty, and Harris wrote a detailed story treatment in a harried two week window, which became the blueprint for the full screenplay. "When we first got the draft down on paper, we knew it really worked." says Harris. "It was an exciting breath of fresh air in a world of super hero movies that have lately explored the same themes." The first draft evolved into thirty subsequent drafts, a new one coming every few weeks until the final day of shooting. "The script is constantly evolving, always changing -- because we all believe that if it ever slows down, we're missing a chance to make it better."

Superman has been popular throughout multiple generations, and audiences always find something in the character to which they can relate. "When [Superman] was created he became a symbol of hope," says Dougherty. "And I think that's why he's endured over the years. The character will always be there. Because he represents what's good in human beings at large; when people seek out Superman they want to see something that makes them believe in the world again."

smallville homecoming

Smallville, not Krypton, is Superman's true home. Martha Kent and her husband Jonathan discovered young Kal-El in a Kansas field, where the smoking, black scar burned into the landscape by his crashed baby pod advertised his otherworldly origins. It is his upbringing in Smallville that grounds Superman, and inspires him to promote the ideals of truth, justice, and the American way.

On the Kent family farm, Clark can relax and be his true self after his five-year interstellar journey. Although it is a welcoming place, in keeping with the theme of *Superman Returns*, it soon becomes apparent that life moves on, even in Smallville.

Superman's return to Earth – specifically Smallville, Kansas – startles Martha Kent. After five long years away, she sometimes doubted that she would see her son again. Superman's smoldering spaceship lands in a dramatic way, thereby signaling to Martha that her son is finally home.

EXT. CORNFIELD – CRATER

Martha rushes along the trench, following SHARDS OF CRYSTAL DEBRIS, until she comes upon a SMOKING CRATER. The smoke clears and she sees it:

SUPERMAN'S SHIP, or what's left. A large charred fuselage surrounded by broken pieces, still glowing from the heat of re-entry. A similar sight to the day he first arrived.

Martha Kent cradles her beloved son in the flaming debris of Superman's crash-landing. She knows she must get him home and let him rest after his long journey.

ung Clark Kent discovers where he came from — and what destiny lies ahead for him. Discovering the spaceship that
ught him to Earth and Jor-El's father crystal, Clark knows it is time to ask his adoptive parents some big questions.

Wire rigging and lots of practice in a harness allow Stephan Bender to take flight and superspeed through vibrant green cornfields as young Clark Kent.

The day young Clark Kent discovered he could fly changed everything. In order to convincingly capture this moment, it took precise timing and collaboration between director, actor, and crew.

Eva Marie Saint, veteran of cinema classics including *North by Northwest* and *On the Waterfront*, plays Clark's adoptive mother, Martha Kent. She is the first one to greet her son upon his return to Earth, and helps acclimate him to a world half a decade removed from where he left it. "Of course she missed him and worried about him, but her life went on," says Saint. "That's what I really liked about the character. She's still an attractive, vital lady. She's not going to sit around baking pies. That's really difficult, I'm sure, for a child to come home and find that everything isn't the status quo."

Because *Superman Returns* was filmed in Australia, the Smallville scenes would not be shot in Kansas. Bryan Singer and his crew, faced with the need to recreate the American Great Plains in the Land Down Under, transformed the countryside near the town of Tamworth (250 miles outside of Sydney) into the Kent homestead. Five hundred acres of corn took root, meticulously timed so that the stalks would be at their fullest when filming began. The crew also constructed a barn, a silo, the Kent main house, and several support structures to capture the environment of Clark's youth.

The Tamworth location captivated Eva Marie Saint, who describes its sunrises and sunsets as being among the most beautiful in the world. "In the early morning during makeup," she relates, "we would run out of the trailer and watch [the sunrise], and everyone would take photos." She instantly felt at home in the Kent farmhouse. "I walked into it and felt like I had always lived there. Before you start [filming] you send photos of yourself as a younger person, and [the production crew] put in Brandon where my real son was. I walked in, and here's photos of my [movie] family! You really feel that it's your house."

Following his failed expedition to Krypton, Superman arrives at the Kent farm in the middle of the night. The crash site left behind by his exhausted starship is a spectacle of smoke and guttering flames. "That was quite a scene," remembers Saint. "It was like the end of the world. Martha knows what it might be, so when she gets there and sees the crash, she thinks, 'My God, he could have been killed!' So when Clark [approaches her] from behind, she jumps — but she's just so happy to see him."

Superman Returns didn't allow Saint to realize her favorite fantasy, but she's holding out hope for a sequel. "I told Bryan that my dream, Eva Marie's dream, is to fly. If I do the next one, I'll put it in the contract," she jokes. "I want Superman to take his mom flying!"

eva marie saint as martha kent

The Kent farm is as warm and welcoming as a summer day in Kansas. It is here that Clark Kent grew up into the kind, honest man he is today. It is also where he first returns to seek the comfort and wisdom of his adoptive mother, M

EXT. KENT FARM

Clark approaches the cornfield and looks around. The farm
has fallen into disrepair – machinery has rusted, and the field
is overgrown. He breathes in the morning air and kneels
down, running his fingers through the soil...remembering.

The barn on the Kent farm was the site of definitive moments in young Clark's life, and is one of the first places Clark revisits when he returns to Smallville. It is a reminder of somewhat simpler times.

Martha Kent's wise counsel helps put Clark's mind at ease. She knows her son is looking for the direction he was searching for while away from Earth for so long.

Director Bryan Singer gives Brandon Routh (Clark Kent/Superman) direction during the Kent farm location shoot.

Clark discovers years' worth of old **Daily Planet** newspapers in the barn cellar, diligently saved for him by Martha. It is in one of these papers that Lois Lane's article, "Why The World Doesn't Need Superman," appears, making Clark question if his identity as Superman is still relevant in a world that has learned to get along without him.

As the Kansas sun sets, Clark ponders what his next move will be. Should he stay in Smallville or return to Metropolis? Should he take up the mantle of the Man of Steel once more – or does the world truly no longer need him?

part 2: superman

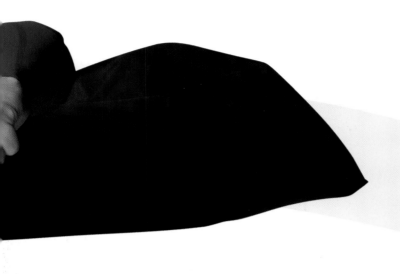

is back

brandon routh as superman/ clark kent

As the central character of the film, Superman fills the role of the archetypal hero. As an Iowa native who tops out at 6'2 3/4", Brandon Routh fits the bill. Routh, who has appeared on soap operas and TV sitcoms but is a relative newcomer to film, grew up a fan of the character, spending many lazy Saturdays of his boyhood clad in Superman pajamas.

Stepping into the Man of Steel's boots was a daunting task, considering the manner in which the late Christopher Reeve defined the character for a generation. "With every respect to Chris and everyone that has gone before me, there's no way I could be what they were," admits Routh. "But I definitely take part of their performances with me, as George Reeves and Kirk Alyn were a part of Christopher Reeve's role. It's fantasy, so you can't help but have all of these [performances], layer upon layer, from the very beginning. I'm just adding my layer."

The shoot was often grueling. To play Superman, Routh had to squeeze into a too-small costume, maintain a strict diet so he didn't gain or lose a single pound during filming, and sweat his way through an extremely physical shoot, with much of it spent suspended from wires in a flight harness.

"There were many days when I was hanging there asking myself, 'Am I really an actor, or am I an athlete?'" says Routh, referring to the flying sequences under the guidance of stunt coordinator R.A. Rondell. "Those [flying] shots are so tedious, since there are so many things that are taken into account — camera angles, the way my hair is flying, cape movement, all these things. There were times when I was doing the right thing, but ten other things had to come in line. It took a lot of patience, waiting for magic to happen."

When he won the role, Routh didn't just sign on to play Superman. He also needed to convey Clark Kent, a challenge eased by Routh's natural persona. "Physically he was born to play Superman," says Routh's co-star Kate

Bosworth, "but his personality is so exceptionally like Clark Kent that it's wonderful. When you talk to him, he's just so soft-spoken, kind, and shy, and he knows these random facts about random things that you'd think Clark Kent would come up with. For example, he told me that the platypus is the only mammal that lays eggs out of the blue one day."

Drawing on his own life experience came in handy, since *Superman Returns* required Routh to portray no less than three separate characters: "True Clark" as seen on the Kent farm; "Clumsy Clark" used to divert attention from his secret identity among his co-workers at the *Daily Planet*; and Superman, a larger-than-life public hero.

"Clark on the farm I always referred to as Kal-El," says Routh, referring to the character's Kryptonian name. "That's the only time he's the Last Son of Krypton. There's only his mother there, and although she calls him Clark, that's his true self. Kal-El/Clark was a lot of my true nature. Clark [at the *Daily Planet*] is a bit of a goofy, overly eager person, who's just a lot of fun to play because everything's so exciting. Life is exciting, and meeting Lois is so exciting that maybe you're dropping things because you can't control your body. That was a part of me too, because I'm a klutz in real life. Superman was the most challenging, because you're becoming someone superhuman. [In real life] we don't do that — we slouch, we do a lot of things that are not very heroic. That took a lot of imagining, and getting in touch with my best intentions."

Routh couldn't be more enthusiastic about Singer's vision for *Superman Returns*. "It's not a 'comic book' movie," he says. "It's a movie [that] happens to be about comic book characters, but it takes this fantastical character and makes it as real as it [can] come across. I'm extremely excited and so proud of everybody."

Superman's costume is the original and most recognizable of all super hero designs. Patterned in the primary colors of red, yellow, and blue, its clinginess shows off Superman's physical strength, while its high boots and flowing cape add a touch of majesty. Superman is one of the few super heroes who doesn't wear a mask. In fact, the closest he comes to a disguise are the glasses he wears as Clark Kent.

Over the last fifteen years, various potential Superman directors have made stabs at reinterpreting the Man of Steel. Bryan Singer always wanted a classic look. That meant no molded plastic muscles — just a simple suit that would be instantly recognizable to anyone who had grown up with the character.

Some updating was required to make the suit visually interesting to the degree that audiences would expect. Costume designer Louise Mingenbach worked with Bryan Singer on the upgrade, sticking to the basics with subtle expressions of panache.

Most noticeable is the chest insignia. Although the S-shield is much smaller than on previous versions, it's in keeping with the size of the "S" in the early comics. As a sculpted medallion, the emblem is a modern enhancement over traditional screen-printing. Difficult to see, but present nonetheless, are the hundreds of tiny "S" shapes laser-cut into the insignia's background.

The costume's colors are another change. The suit has a darker sheen than previous versions, with a deeper blue, a less vibrant yellow, and a red that approaches maroon. Superman's cape is made of a heavy material that gives it form and weight, and lacks any "S" embellishment (a concession to the visual effects department, since a yellow logo on the flapping red cape would look distracting during flight sequences).

The suit is made from milliskin, a synthetic material that is thin but extremely tight. Routh compared wearing the skintight costume to wearing a rubber band. Mingenbach arranged for Routh to wear subtle muscle padding beneath the costume to restore the muscular definition that had been squeezed out by the milliskin.

Superman's boots have always given him the rakish look of a swashbuckler. In *Superman Returns*, the thick red leather of the boots is laser-cut with tiny "S" insignias, and each boot boasts a thick sole as a visual counterbalance to Brandon Routh's broad shoulders. Decorating the heel and sole of each boot are more "S" insignias.

Many different versions of the suit came out of the costume department — more than 60 in all. Stunt versions lacked excess embellishments. Water versions had colors that would not darken when doused by liquid. Arms-up suits possessed extra-long sleeves, to prevent Routh's wrists from popping out whenever he assumed Superman's classic flying pose. Relatively rare "hero suits" are the ones seen in close-ups and studio publicity shots.

superman's
costume

RED SUN
preliminary design

Superman's costume would not be complete without the iconic S-shield emblazoned across his chest. In **Superman Returns**, this motif is extended to his belt buckle and other costume details, such as his boots and even his gray pod suit.

This painting by Alex Ross was inspiration for an exciting scene in *Superman Returns*.

The journey to Krypton and back took five years — long enough for a cooped-up Superman to be aching to test his mettle once more. Once on Earth, he gets back into his super-heroic groove with a series of dazzling feats. The world quickly takes notice: the Man of Steel is back!

Superman's most spectacular exploit, the one that marks his return to public adulation, is his role in stopping the death plunge of an out-of-control Boeing 777 press jet. After his debut, Superman flies into action against threats both major and minor. A signature moment comes during an urban rooftop standoff. When crooks terrorize the street-level police cordon with a tripod-mounted machine gun, Superman shows up to shut them down. As he strides forward into the path of automatic gunfire, bullets zing off his chest in bright streaks in a classic display of power. In the next moment, the scene is ratcheted up still further when a handgun slug ricochets harmlessly off of Superman's eyeball.

superman's super-feats

A dramatic event—the first privately funded launch of a space shuttle. This key dramatic sequence promises lots of action and suspense, especially for Lois Lane and the press aboard the aircraft attached to the shuttle.

INT. JET – PRESS CABIN

Lois and the others feel the jet rattle and lurch forward. Bobbie-Faye is thrown to the floor. People scream, pinned to their seats as they're hit by pounding g-forces. THE ROAR of the BOOSTERS and the sound of BUCKLING METAL are DEAFENING.

The burning Boeing 777 jet plummets rapidly toward a terrified crowd in a packed baseball stadium. The crowds' cries of fear turn quickly to deafening roars of joy once they realize that Superman has returned — and in a very big way!

INT. JET — PRESS CABIN

Stunned passengers slowly look up from their sea
They hear the sound of GROANING METAL as THE DO
IS RIPPED FROM ITS HINGES and tossed aside. The yel
rescue slide inflates, and Superman steps inside.

SUPERMAN
Is everyone alright?

*Disaster occurs when the Boeing 777 jet Lois Lane is onboard does
separate from the Explorer shuttle piggybacked to it. As Lois begins to
that this will be the last news story she ever files, Superman makes
reappearance known, embarking on his first heroic challenge in five ye*

part 3: *metropolis's*

DAILY

favorite son

metropolis

Metropolis has played a part in the Superman universe since 1939, when it first appeared by name in the pages of a comic book. Modeled in part on Joe Shuster's birthplace of Cleveland, Ohio and his childhood home of Toronto, Ontario, Metropolis is better recognized as an alternate depiction of New York City.

The comparisons become obvious when the Metropolis of *Superman Returns* is viewed from the air. Skyscrapers jut upward like needles in a pincushion, surrounded on all sides by waterways and busy harbors. This vibrant east coast urban center is the nexus of Superman's world. Even the schemes of Lex Luthor, while global in scale, have their most damaging effects on Metropolis, when the tremors caused by the raising of New Krypton shake the mighty city to its foundations.

As befits a city with a rich history, Metropolis boasts an eclectic profile made up of buildings from every era. Modern glass-and-steel towers stand alongside proud pre-war constructions of brick. Metropolis is a vibrant community that has preserved its past, a philosophy that mirrors Bryan Singer's approach to *Superman Returns*. The buildings of the Metropolis skyline are signposts to earlier incarnations of the Superman legend, including the '30s, the '50s, the '70s, and today.

Superman has a day job. As Clark Kent, senior reporter for Metropolis's *Daily Planet* newspaper, he stays plugged into news feeds, scanning unfolding events for anything that looks like a job for Superman. The Planet offices are also where he met his true love, Lois Lane. When Clark Kent comes back to the Planet after a five-year absence, every moment is a painful reminder of the life he could have had.

The *Daily Planet* is Metropolis's preeminent newspaper, and home to Superman's roster of supporting characters. In *Superman Returns*, this includes familiar faces such as editor-in-chief Perry White, and staff photographer Jimmy Olsen, as well as newcomer Richard White (Perry's nephew and Lois's fiancée).

The *Daily Planet* is based in a commanding edifice that has been standing since 1932, if the logo embedded into the lobby floor is any guide. As befits a building of that period, it is designed in classic American art deco. Its adornments — including the rams' heads outside Perry White's window and the stone warriors looking out on the Planet's exterior plaza — bear the streamlined contours of deco design. Other telltale influences include the radiating sunbursts that panel the elevator walls, and the zigzagging patterns that add visual zest to the building's decorative windows.

the daily planet

The Daily Planet building is a fittingly impressive testament to the pursuit of truth and justice. It has stood proudly in Metropolis since its construction in 1932.

The Art Deco exterior gives way to very modern offices and a state-of-the art bullpen. The marriage of form and function is a perfect complement to the elegance and sophistication of the most famous building in Metropolis.

In most of his previous incarnations, *Daily Planet* editor-in-chief Perry White has been the archetypal tough-talking boss. *Superman: The Movie*, which cast veteran actor Jackie Cooper in the role, presented a Perry White who barked commands at the staff and repeatedly warned Jimmy Olsen, "Don't call me Chief!"

But Frank Langella, who plays Perry White in *Superman Returns*, says that his interpretation of the character "couldn't be further away" from that pugnacious prototype. "From the very first day, Bryan was very clear that he wanted Perry White [to be] the anchor of the film," he says. "Not brash, not cigar-chomping, not a finger-pointing yeller, but actually a man who wants to protect his paper against everything else. So we went away from any of the other clichēs you may have seen."

Langella is himself a forty-year veteran of film and television. He arrived at the *Superman Returns* set in Australia immediately after wrapping work on the George Clooney drama *Good Night and Good Luck*, and praises the experience of working with Bryan Singer. "Bryan is a true mad genius," he says. "He has the entire movie in his head moment to moment, and you can literally see it change as he's standing there. Bryan is a stream of consciousness director, in that everything he's thinking — positive negative, confused, clear — all those things come out of his mouth. It's like a tape is running constantly. If you trust him, and I do implicitly, eventually he finds exactly what he wants."

Langella worked closely with the actors chosen to portray the *Daily Planet* staff, including Brandon Routh (Clark Kent), Kate Bosworth (Lois Lane), Sam Huntington (Jimmy Olsen), and James Marsden (Richard White). Faced with a team of relative youngsters, Langella quickly discovered that he had become the elder statesman. "These are basically four actors who are all thirty or forty years younger than me," he says. "They were really remarkably gentlemanly and ladylike people. There weren't any divas on the set." As evidence, he points to Brandon Routh, a newcomer to film who remained unfailingly polite throughout the shoot. "Brandon got over 'Sir' and 'Mister Langella' after the first couple days," he says, "when I said, 'We're going to be together for four months, so just stop!'"

frank langella as perry white

Perry White in action. Direct and pragmatic, Perry demands much from his staff, especially his best reporters like Lois Lane and intrepid photographer Jimmy Olsen. Never one to shy away from a news story no matter how controversial, Perry is responsible for guiding the **Daily Planet** into the cutting edge of the 21st century.

Clark Kent's return to Metropolis and life at the Daily Planet does not go as smoothly as he had hoped. While some things have managed to stay the same, Clark is crestfallen to discover that Lois Lane has moved on with her life and has a young son – and a fiancée.

INT. DAILY PLANET — ELEVATOR BANK

WE FOLLOW two suitcases OVER the large *Daily Planet* emblem on the floor, INTO:

THE DAILY PLANET BULLPEN — CONTINUOUS ACTION

Reporters, assistants, and copy boys scurry about. RINGING PHONES. TELEVISIONS tuned to NEWS CHANNELS.

We CONTINUE TO FOLLOW the SUITCASES THROUGH the bullpen, clumsily knocking into one desk after another. People try to avoid them.

THE SUITCASES hit a particular desk and a CAMERA falls toward the ground. IN THE BLINK OF AN EYE, the camera is caught with one hand by:

CLARK KENT. Now wearing glasses and a suit.

Lois and Richard kiss. Clark shifts, uncomfortable.

Clark gently clears his throat.

LOIS
Oh! This is Clark. Richard, Clark. Clark, Richard.
(to Clark)
Richard's an assistant editor here who's
basically saved our international section.
He's also a pilot, and he likes horror movies.
(to Richard)
Clark is...well, Clark.

Jimmy Olsen is perhaps the only one truly thrilled at Clark's return, for he has always looked up to the older reporter as a big brother figure. Clark, on the other hand, must deal with the new love in Lois's life, Richard White. But what are Lois's feelings for Superman after all this time?

Jimmy Olsen is the *Daily Planet*'s staff photographer, known for his red hair, his bow tie, and his irrepressible enthusiasm. In the comic books, Jimmy wears a signal watch given to him by Superman so that he can signal for danger at any moment. From 1954-1974, the character even rated a comic book series of his own, entitled *Superman's Pal, Jimmy Olsen*.

"When I was a little boy I was such a ridiculous Superman fan," says Sam Huntington, the actor chosen to play Jimmy Olsen in *Superman Returns*. "For me, this was probably the coolest job that I could have ever gotten. I've always had a special connection with the character."

Huntington feels a kinship with Jimmy, believing that the character's spirited personality is an echo of Huntington's own. "He's an eager to please, naïve, innocent, happy guy," he says. "His cup is half-full. I really respect people like that, since you see it so little these days."

1978's *Superman: The Movie* put Marc McClure in the role of Jimmy Olsen, but McClure was just one in a long line of actors that included Tommy Bond in the 1940s movie serials and Jack Larson in the 1950s TV show, *The Adventures of Superman*. As an homage to the work of previous creators, and as an Easter egg for eagle-eyed fans, director Bryan Singer cast Larson as the bartender at the working-class Metropolis boxers' bar, the Ace O'Clubs.

"It was bizarre," says Huntington. "I had never seen any of the TV shows. I had studied the Mark McClure portrayal before I came on to this film, so it was really interesting to meet [Larson], to throw other bits of his personality into my [own] take. I have the sensibility of everyone who has portrayed the character, while at the same time bringing my own sense of humor to the table."

Huntington expresses such an enthusiasm for the opportunity that he can't help but sound more than a little like Jimmy. "When I got the phone call that I'd gotten the job, it was such an amazing feeling, like I had won the Super Bowl," he says. *Superman Returns* is all the better for the choice.

sam huntington as jimmy olsen

Richard White, Perry's nephew, is a top-notch reporter and a good father to Lois's son. Try as he might, Clark cannot fault Richard for loving Lois as he does.

Lois Lane's adorable son Jason, played by Tristan Leabu, is a very smart and precocious five-year-old. Despite his many allergies and somewhat frail appearance, Jason is truly as brave and fearless as his mother.

"I was very much aware of the magnitude of this character, which is why I chose to approach it as a fresh start. For me, it was important to create a new Lois Lane." That's Kate Bosworth, speaking of her role in *Superman Returns* as the brassy ace of the Daily Planet bullpen, star reporter Lois Lane. Though Lois once shared a relationship with Superman, she has since moved on and is raising her five-year-old son with her fiancée, Richard White.

Bosworth, star of such films as *Blue Crush* and *Beyond the Sea*, plays a Lois who is half a decade older than the version of the character conceived for the original films. That time gap, coupled with Lois's transition into motherhood, gives the impression of a woman in her mid-30s. Bosworth, twenty-two at the time of filming, brought a maturity to the role despite her chronological age.

"I'm not a mother," allows Bosworth, "but I assume that priorities shift less on oneself and more on the little thing that you've created. And that was where I maintained my focus — on my child. I think this Lois cares more about her child than she does herself, which is a big leap for any woman to make. When you're a young woman and you're gung-ho and motivated, you're thinking of your career. And when you bring a child into the world, you're forced to mature."

In 2004's *Beyond the Sea*, Bosworth acted opposite Kevin Spacey as Sandra Dee to his Bobby Darin. Winning a role in *Superman Returns* allowed her to work with Spacey a second time, and her prior experience (which she describes as a "beautiful familiarity") helped calm her nerves. "I was so nervous coming to work every day because we were working on Superman," she says. "I think if I hadn't worked with Kevin before, and I didn't know him as well as I did, I would have been shaking in my boots."

In keeping with the design scheme of Metropolis, much of Lois's wardrobe has a timeless 1940s feel, thanks to the input of costume designer Louise Mingenbach. "I got to fly to Sydney early and, with Louise, create [Lois's] look," says Bosworth. "Because we're creating such a classic original look, everything had to be original. You couldn't buy it off the rack."

Lois's most striking outfit is the retro-styled gown she wears aboard the *Gertrude* yacht, donned for a Pulitzer award ceremony that is quickly forgotten as Lex Luthor's schemes take center stage. "[Louise and I] were going through racks and racks of 1920s, 1930s, and 1940s outfits," remembers Bosworth. "There was one dress that was just hideous, bright yellow with a bright red sash. I tried it on, and by erasing the horrid color, the shape was right." Bosworth's eye for form resulted in a formal, arresting outfit possessing what she calls a "tuxedo-like" look.

Unfortunately, playing Lois left little time for the pleasures of costume selection. The character has always been a scrapper who would do anything for a story, and Bosworth endured several grueling sequences under the eye of stunt coordinator R.A. Rondell. Inside a moving gimbal that simulated the pantry of the *Gertrude* yacht, she suffered repeated dunkings in a tank of water. A much larger gimbal supported the entire set of the Boeing 777 jet interior. Its passengers, including Bosworth, were rocked to the edge of airsickness. "One of my biggest phobias is crashing in an airplane," says Bosworth, "so it was basically like playing out your nightmare."

kate bosworth as lois lane

Two sides of Lois Lane: ace reporter and loving mother. As much as Lois loves doggedly pursuing a good news story, it is quality time spent with her son Jason that truly makes her happy.

Lois Lane is a woman of many talents and abilities, but it will take all her internal strength to deal with her feelings for Superman now that he is back. Lois's love for her son Jason is her touchstone during the rough times ahead.

LOIS
Hey, can I ask you something?

CLARK
Sure.

LOIS
Have you ever been in love?

Clark almost starts to answer.

LOIS
Or at least...have you ever met
someone and it's almost like you
were from totally different worlds,
but you share such a strong connection
that you knew you were destined to be
with each other? But then he takes off withou
explaining why, or without even
saying goodbye?

In **Superman Returns**, the classic love triangle between Lois Lane and Clark Kent/Superman becomes even more complicated. Superman's long absence and sudden return has only added new layers of tension.

Bryan Singer directs Brandon Routh in a key dramatic sequence.

Clark Kent races through the crowded streets of Metropolis in search of a quiet place to make the transition into Superman.

Superman and Lois Lane are one of the great couples of fiction. In the original *Superman: The Movie*, it is Lois's drive for a story that initially puts the two together. Yet after a rendezvous on Lois's penthouse balcony, followed by a magical flight through the Metropolis night sky, the two realize that they belong to each other.

However, the cruel truth of *Superman Returns* is that love doesn't always wait. Superman, in an effort to discover the secrets of his birthworld, left Earth without saying goodbye to the woman who meant so much to him.

While he was gone, Lois wrote a Pulitzer Prize-winning story, "Why the World Doesn't Need Superman." As soon as he returns, Superman runs head-first into the implications of that statement. Lois has moved on without him. She has a five-year-old son, Jason, and a fiancée, Richard White.

This made things tough for actor James Marsden, who plays Richard. Being cast as Superman's romantic rival meant that the audience would be rooting against him, even though Richard White is written as a likeable person who does nothing to invite hostility. "Everyone knows who Superman is, and everyone knows who Lois Lane is," he says. "We want to see them together. The challenge for me was to make [Richard] as likeable as possible, so that this situation is as difficult for her as possible."

He adds, "I think it mimics what real life is like. It would be easier if there was a definite good guy and definite bad guy, because it would make everyone's decisions a lot easier, but I've never encountered that."

Like Kevin Spacey, Marsden is a veteran of previous Bryan Singer films. In *X-Men* and *X2: X-Men United*, he led the titular team as the optic-blasting mutant Cyclops. Yet, having gained fame as a super hero, Marsden believes that portraying a regular guy is far more relaxing. "I love playing Cyclops, but as a normal human being, I'm not super at all," he says. "It was much more comfortable to be playing Richard White. Both literally, to wear suits as opposed to black leather, and figuratively, because I see myself more as Richard than I do as Cyclops."

Marsden considers Richard a real-world version of Superman. "He can't compete with [Superman's] superpowers, but if you were to pick one person who's the most like him, it's Richard. I think [Lois] loves both of them in different ways. Right now I'm the emotional kryptonite."

Richard White is a new character in the Superman canon, so where does he go from here? Marsden confesses that he doesn't know what may lie in store, but speculates that the seeds planted in *Superman Returns* could allow the character to go in any direction in subsequent films. "He could do a 180 and become a villain," says Marsden, "because this jealousy [of Superman] crescendos. Or it can be something they [continue to] struggle with."

the love triangle:

james marsden as richard white

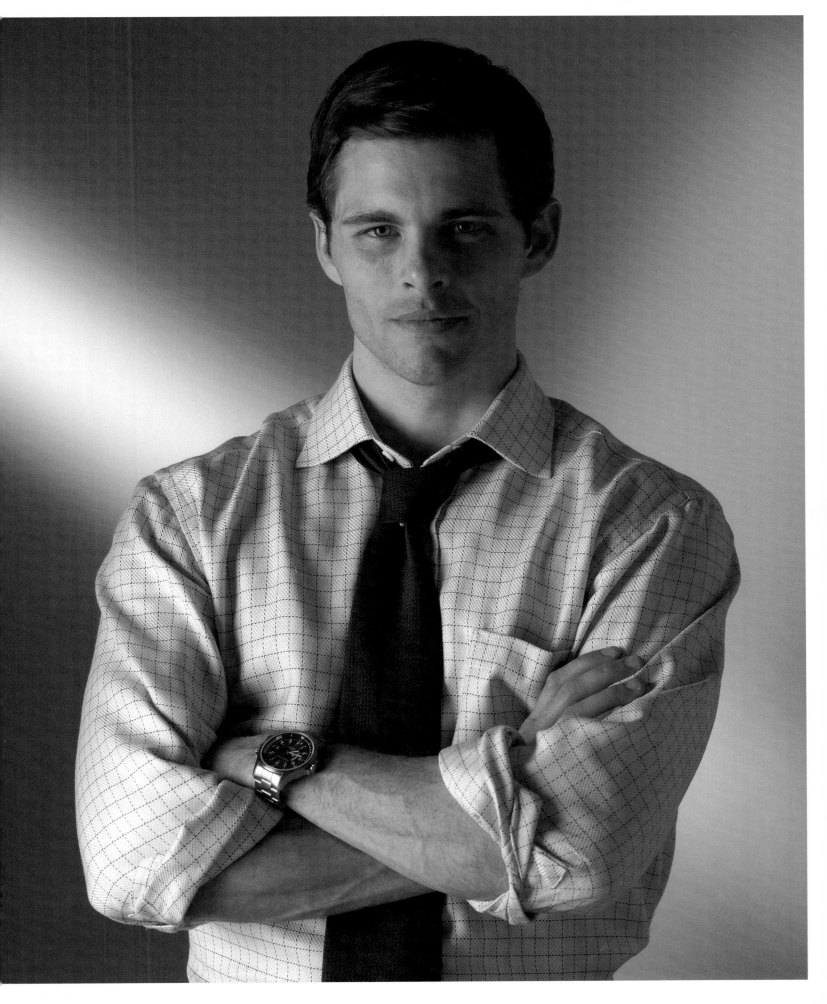

. DAILY PLANET – ROOFTOP

THEY LAND gently on the roof. Lois looks deeply into his eyes, faces just inches apart. They both can see it coming. This is the moment. Lois begins to MOVE CLOSER – and just as her lips are about to touch his...Lois abruptly pulls away.

...neras, green screen, and genuine screen chemistry all help to capture a tender moment between Lois Lane
...d Superman. Despite conflicted emotions and hurt feelings, the love between these two is evident and pure.

part 4: old enemy,

new krypton

lex luthor's
return

Lex Luthor is Superman's opposite number, and has been the perfect foil for the Man of Steel since his comic book introduction in 1940. Lex's key character trait is his intellect, which he applies to the acquisition of unspeakable wealth and the domination of everyone who surrounds him. To Lex, Superman is a wild card with the power to topple his criminal schemes through raw strength alone.

Lex isn't the kind of enemy that Superman punches. To Lex, true combat occurs on a cerebral plane, and he is a master at outthinking his opponents. "That's the beauty of Lex; that it's the classic Man versus Superman," says screenwriter Dougherty. "He is a man of vast intellect and power, and in his mind Superman represents something that is a threat to humanity. In Lex's mind he's doing us a favor by getting rid of Superman. It's a great conflict to see vast intellect versus great strength."

This dynamic of brain against brawn has been expressed in many forms throughout the character's history. In his original embodiment, Lex was a super scientist whose diabolical inventions nearly caused the death of the Man of Steel. The character later evolved into the CEO of a multinational business conglomerate, but lost none of his bloodthirsty edge. In 1978's *Superman: The Movie*, Gene Hackman took to the role with relish, updating the part with splashes of humor. *Superman Returns* restores the risk to Luthor, retaining elements of the original with a new sheen of menace.

Academy Award-winning actor Kevin Spacey plays Lex Luthor, infusing the role with gravity and bite. Spacey, star of such acclaimed films as *American Beauty* and *L.A. Confidential*, shares a history with *Superman Returns* director Bryan Singer. Spacey played Roger "Verbal" Kint in Singer's first major feature, *The Usual Suspects*.

Unlike Gene Hackman, who reportedly refused to shave his head for *Superman: The Movie* and appeared wearing a bald skullcap only briefly, Spacey went full-out and sported a razor-smooth pate. Spacey discourages further comparisons to Hackman, stating he never intended to channel any previous performances of Luthor. "I just thought that was a mistake, to decide, 'I'm going to be just like Gene Hackman,'" he says. "The character is the character, so you try to honor the character."

In *Superman Returns*, Lex has an edge. Much less comic than he appeared in his prior film incarnation, he is keenly aware of his previous humiliations at Superman's hands and has decided to raise the stakes. "While he's a character that still has a comic flair, this is a much darker Lex," says Spacey. "This is a bitter Lex. This is a Lex out for revenge."

When Spacey signed on for *The Usual Suspects*, Bryan Singer was virtually unknown as a director. In the ten years since then, Singer has helmed several blockbusters and established a reputation as a master at super-heroic sci-fi. Despite the time gap, Spacey says that reuniting with Singer on *Superman Returns* wasn't very different at all.

"Bryan is the same man he was then," says Spacey. "In a lot of ways it was like no time had gone by. It was enlightening to see how much he's advanced as a filmmaker. He has all these remarkable tools at his disposal now, much different [than on *The Usual Suspects*] when we made a little $5 million movie."

It was, in fact, Spacey's respect for Singer that first drew him to the project. "I think if Bryan hadn't been directing this movie I wouldn't have done it," he says. "It's as simple as that. I've never done a movie like that before, but there are a lot of reasons why I'm glad I did it. He assembled a terrific team and a great cast, and the writers did a wonderful job on the script."

kevin spacey as lex luthor

the vanderworth *fortune*

Determined that his wealth should rival his intellect, Lex Luthor hatches an elaborate plan that will allow him to fund his plans for world domination. He decides to pursue the oldest avenue to instant wealth — marry into money. The death of Gertrude Vanderworth leaves Lex the sole heir to the multi-billion dollar Vanderworth shipping fortune, and he inherits a mansion on the Metropolis shorefront which becomes a headquarters for villainy.

Conceptual design for the mansion relied heavily on flamboyant ornamentation, since the Vanderworths had been conceived as the type of people who valued money over style. Greco-Roman sculptures and Renaissance paintings share the same space in an eclectic atmosphere of cluttered excess. Gertrude Vanderworth's prized lap dogs make their presence known in tacky oil paintings, which hang on the mansion walls while the real pooches yap underfoot.

In the mansion's basement lies a mind-boggling model railroad. Built by the late Mr. Vanderworth, an obsessive hobbyist, the railroad features miniaturized replicas of everything from the Swiss Alps to Metropolis, separated by loops and whorls of endless track. The railroad set comes in handy when Lex Luthor experiments with the potency of Kryptonian crystal growth. Unfortunately for the model railroad, it does not survive the demonstration.

The *Gertrude* yacht is the most important asset possessed by Lex. Complete with a swimming pool and a helicopter landing pad, the *Gertrude* is a beautiful, elegant vessel that is appropriated by Lex as a mobile command center. Reflections from the water below shine through the yacht's glass bottom while Lex and Kitty Kowalski argue over strategy.

The train set in the basement of the Vanderworth mansion is the setting for the beginning of Lex Luthor's plan for the defeat of Superman. It is here that he puts his theory of Kryptonian technology to the test.

The Gertrude contains many state-of-the art rooms, including a fully stocked library, a spacious study, and a gourmet kitchen and pantry. All of these amenities are needed to keep Lex Luthor happy and sated on his long trip to the Arctic.

Lex Luthor is a mad genius whose undeniable charm and willingness to sacrifice billions makes him a formidable foe. Lex's years in jail have left him itching for revenge, and have led to the formation of his most sinister plan yet.

Lois and her son Jason's capture by Lex Luthor on the Gertrude yacht leads to start...
revelations and new peril for the plucky reporter and her son. The question is ...
Superman arrive in time to save the day – or suffer defeat at the hand of the evil Luth...

LOIS
Wait a minute. This was the Vanderworth's yacht. Gertrude Vanderworth's brother-in-law...

LEX
...is a Federal Court of Appeals judge. You know, Superman's good at catching criminals, but he's not much on Miranda rights, due process, that sort of thing.

Lois processes the information.

LOIS
Did you have anything to do with the blackout?

Lex's eyes light up.

LEX
Are you fishing for an interview, Miss Lane?

LOIS
It's been awhile since you were a headline. Maybe it's time people knew your name again. *(pulling Jason closer)*
How about we turn the boat around, call a cab for my son... and then you can do whatever you want with me.

*Trapped in the pantry aboard **The Gertrude**, Lois and Jason find themselves in a dire situation. With New Krypton rapidly expanding and Superman already busy, Lois and her son will have to rely on their own bravery and quick wits.*

INT. FORTRESS OF SOLITUDE

They cautiously enter the Fortress, gawking. It's composed of a large central chamber, with smaller adjoining rooms.

> **LEX**
> *(whispers)*
> Possibilities...possibilities...

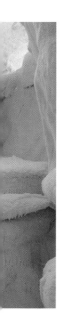

Lex Luthor and his motley crew enter Superman's arctic Fortress of Solitude in search of answers. It is here that Lex discovers the key to his master plan.

After Lex Luthor divines the location of Superman's Fortress of Solitude, he steers the *Gertrude* far north of the Arctic Circle. Upon arrival, Lex and his followers set off on a punishing journey over a glacial landscape, eventually discovering an offshoot crystal connected to the root of Superman's Fortress of Solitude. This marker leads Lex to the genuine item, where he discovers everything he ever wanted to know about crystals — in the process learning how to make his real-estate scheme a reality.

To simulate the wintry approach to the Fortress of Solitude, the *Superman Returns* crew designed a winding set dressed with foam-sprayed artificial snow and icicles of clear plastic. The sparkling white polar set, shot on a soundstage in Fox Studios Sydney, earned the nickname "Santa's Grotto."

The Fortress of Solitude very closely mirrored the design established by *Superman: The Movie* production designer John Barry in the 1970s. In that film, the Fortress constructed itself after Clark Kent threw a crystal "seed" into the soft arctic snow. *Superman Returns* production designer Guy Dyas intentionally recreated the Barry design to the best of his abilities.

The Fortress of Solitude adheres to the fundamental rules of Kryptonian design — clean, sterile, and linear. It is made up of translucent crystalline columns that glow with an inner light, many of them as thick as redwood trunks. Everything in the Fortress, including the control panel that operates holographic recordings, is composed of crystals. The ability of Kryptonian minerals to replicate and form themselves into complex structures is key to the plot of *Superman Returns*, and is exploited by Lex Luthor during the creation of New Krypton.

the fortress of
solitude

EXT. ARCTIC SKIES

VWOOSH! Superman soars through a dark and overcast sky. TIGHT on his face — we begin to hear...

SUPERMAN (V.O.)
Father...

NORTHERN LIGHTS shimmer in the gray sky. Superman soars through them...

SUPERMAN (V.O.)
It's been a long time since I've come to you...

...and moves toward something in the distance...

SUPERMAN (V.O.)
But I've never felt so alone.

Superman stands on the steps of the Fortress of Solitude, ready to seek council with the spirit of his Kryptonian father, Jor

Kitty Kowalski is Lex Luthor's love interest and partner-in-crime, based in part on Miss Teschmacher, played by Valerie Perrine in 1978's *Superman: The Movie*. Parker Posey, who plays Kitty, is mostly known for her roles in critically-admired independent films such as *Best in Show* and *A Mighty Wind*. *Superman Returns* represents Posey's first step into the realm of summer blockbusters.

"It will be the part that I've played that most people will see," admits Posey. "[Screenwriters] Dan [Harris] and Mike [Dougherty] wrote it with me in mind. When I got this offer it was kind of unexpected, [but] I immediately thought, wow, what an opportunity."

Posey prepped for the role by researching *Superman: The Movie*. She determined that Lex's relationships with his women were doomed to dysfunction, based on a lack of mutual respect. Nevertheless, she says, "[Kitty's] a romantic. She fell in love with Lex, and fell in love with the lifestyle."

Kitty is stuck in a bad relationship with a man who is willing to kill millions. Despite Lex's genocidal aims, Parker feels that, at least initially, Kitty believes that he's not that bad at heart. "I don't think she's conscious of what she's doing," she explains. "She's with a man who loves himself more than he loves her. She waits for him to be the good guy she saw when she fell in love with him. There's that kind of longing."

Posey found acting opposite Kevin Spacey to be a challenging experience. "He was my Lex Luthor," she admits. "I stay in character a lot when I work, and he does as well. He's got a great edge. He's an intense guy, and he's very dedicated and talented."

During the course of *Superman Returns*, Kitty Kowalski develops the first glimmers of a conscience while in the presence of the Man of Steel. "She has a real transformation," says Posey, speculating on her character's next move should the film spawn sequels. "By the end of the movie you're going to wonder what's going to happen, if she's going to do something to Lex to stop him."

parker posey as kitty kowalski

The wily and style-conscious Kitty has a fondness for fashion and pooches, although her rescue from potential death leaves her with a new and growing admiration for Superman and his principles.

new krypton

Lex Luthor has always had an obsession with real estate. In *Superman Returns*, he steals the secrets of Kryptonian crystal technology from the Fortress of Solitude, then uses that knowledge to create an eighth continent in the middle of the Atlantic. Lex dubs this continent New Krypton.

Structurally, New Krypton is similar to other Kryptonian features, possessing the unnaturally straight lines found in crystal architecture. Yet the island has a more sinister aura, with crystals of smoky gray that multiply menacingly as the expanding landmass of New Krypton threatens to swamp the planet's coastlines. Fault-line tremors triggered by the island's growth are felt as far away as Metropolis, and are powerful enough to topple the globe from atop the Daily Planet building.

New Krypton sets down its roots like a virulent weed, anchoring itself to the sea bed as it threatens to become a permanent part of Earth's topography. Lois Lane and her son Jason, locked aboard Lex Luthor's yacht, the *Gertrude*, experience the pandemonium as the expanding island cracks the earth and roils the sea. Richard White flies in his seaplane to rescue the pair, while Superman prepares for a final showdown with his arch-nemesis.

As Superman steps foot onto New Krypton, he realizes that the eerie doppelganger of his destroyed home world is nothing more t[han] a kryptonite-laced trap. Lex Luthor's new continent threatens to destroy most of the Western hemisphere if it not stopped in time.

Lex Luthor confronts Superman on the dangerous terrain of New Krypton, unleashing a vicious attack on the struggling hero.

superman defeated /
superman triumphant

Superman confronts Lex on the turbulent face of New Krypton, but is weakened by the kryptonite that permeates the very landscape on which he stands. Lex and his thugs unleash a merciless beating on the fallen super hero. With relish, Lex pierces Superman's back with a kryptonite shard, then leaves him for dead in the churning waters at the island's base.

Superman taps his last reserves of strength, and in an unbelievable display of might, launches New Krypton into space. Lex Luthor and Kitty Kowalski escape aboard Lex's helicopter, free to scheme another day.

When a battle-wounded Superman checks in for a stint in Metropolis Hospital, a legion of supporters assembles in the street outside to maintain an around-the-clock vigil. The *Daily Planet* even mocks up a headline, SUPERMAN IS DEAD, to appear in the tragic event of the Man of Steel's passing. But Superman pulls through, emerging stronger on both a physical and a spiritual level. His ordeal has taught him that there *is* a place for a Superman in the world. Though his relationship with Lois Lane is still in flux, Superman has at last found his home.

Marshalling all his incredible strength despite his injuries, Superman manages to dig out New Krypton from its ocean bed and send it hurtling into outer space.

Hundreds gather in Metropolis to wish Superman well, including Martha Kent and Lois Lane, who brings along her son Jason.

Bryan Singer chats with a smiling Kate Bosworth between takes on the Metropolis hospital set.

*S*uperman Returns encompasses three distinct environments — Krypton, Smallville, and Metropolis — each with its own design challenges. The three needed to look utterly different, since the transitions between them would help the audience relate to Superman's journey.

Production designer Guy Dyas, a veteran of Bryan Singer's *X2: X-Men United*, helmed the efforts to create believable and memorable environments. He and his crew churned out reams of sketches, paintings, storyboards, and photo composites, and built set models that existed both as paper-and-glue constructions and as bits-and-bytes assemblages in the virtual world of CG.

The Kent homestead in Smallville, Kansas is wildly different from Krypton. It is here that Kal-El grew up under the name Clark Kent, and it is here that Clark internalized the values that he summarizes as "truth, justice, and the American way." The Kent farm is meant to be a wholesome and welcoming place, suffused with sunlight shining from endless blue skies and surrounded by golden fields of head-high corn. The wide open spaces of Smallville stretch to the far horizon, unlike the confining crystal palaces of Krypton or the concrete canyons of Metropolis.

Metropolis boasts fascinating art deco detailing and other architecture from the early 20th century, mixed in among contemporary structures. If Smallville emphasizes the distant horizon, Metropolis is all about the vertical. Its skyscrapers stretch ever upward, creating artificial valleys that serve as backdrops for Superman's sorties. "It's as though we took a city like Chicago, and then stretched all the skyscrapers upward by another thirty percent," explains Dyas. Metropolis's art deco sleekness expresses itself in the rams-head gargoyles outside Perry White's Daily Planet office and the stained glass zigzag patterns in the Planet building's main lobby. "Stylistically, art deco is a perfect fit for Superman," says Dyas. "It takes its inspiration from the machine age, but it's also an ode to the human body, since it personifies the power of human physical strength."

the world of *superman returns*

Superman: The Movie featured the production designs of John Barry. *Superman Returns* pays homage to Barry's groundbreaking creations from a quarter-century ago, including the design work for the Kent homestead and the Fortress of Solitude. Yet Guy Dyas didn't want a straight recreation of the '78 film. Metropolis, for example, is an entirely new creation that pulls pieces from the 1930s and every subsequent decade, in an effort to acknowledge the roots of a character who has endured for nearly seventy years.

"I've always thought of Superman as the king of comic book heroes," says Dyas, "so from the very start we felt a strong responsibility to be faithful to the character and his various incarnations. In essence we wanted to create a 'classic Superman' film, as opposed to trying to do something like a re-imagining of the character."

The biggest challenge for Dyas's team lay in trying to realize the film's vast scope on a severely compressed timetable. "Originally Bryan and I had started working on another production for Warner Bros., *Logan's Run*," says Dyas, "but halfway through pre-production, the Superman opportunity caused us to completely switch projects within 24 hours." Dyas packed up his tools and moved his entire art department over to the new *Superman Returns* offices, breaking the unwelcome news that they only had eight months before the start of shooting.

Fortunately, the results were exquisite. The film has a timeless feel, incorporating elements from so many eras that it's difficult to pin down as the product of any particular decade. "'Timeless' and 'classic' are adjectives we used to describe the overall feel we wanted to create," says Dyas. "We subtly accentuated certain aspects of the sets and costumes and avoided using anything too much of the moment." As an added benefit, the ageless atmosphere accentuates the film's romantic subplot. The interplay between Lois and Superman is at times reminiscent of the best 1940s romances.

Bringing *Superman Returns* to life required miracles from the departments responsible for visual effects and stunt work. And if the rendering of planetary fragments and continent-swallowing islands weren't enough of a challenge for the visual-effects team they had to face one of the oldest problems in the book — making audiences believe that a man can fly.

Despite Superman's long history on film and television, it's always been tough to sell the illusion of flight. Director Singer is quick to give credit to the sophistication of modern visual effects. "Technology's constantly changing, and with it comes more possibilities," he says. "The things we're doing in this film could not have been done even a year ago."

For some shots, computer artists rendered an entirely digital Superman. This came with its own problems, because audiences are so used to seeing human beings that a badly-rendered CG character will snap their suspension of disbelief. "Our character has hair," laments Singer, ticking off the complications raised by the Man of Steel's minimalist costume. "His face is exposed, and therefore his performance and personality are exposed." Singer's CG artists used state of the art technology to render Superman down to his last hair follicle.

But depicting a man with the abilities of a demigod requires input from many disciplines. "When you're making a Superman movie you have to create the physics of Superman," says Singer. "How much strain does it take to catch a plane in flight, or an automobile? When do you leap and when do you float? What kind of hand motions are used to navigate through the sky?" Working with Brandon Routh, Singer built a set of superhuman physical laws that became part of his directorial palette.

Stunt coordinator R.A. Rondell worked closely with Routh, knowing that the live-action shots of Superman in flight would be crucial to maintaining the illusion. The tools at Rondell's disposal included a variety of wire-suspension flying harnesses, as well as old-fashioned physical training. "I told [Routh] from day one, 'You're going to hate me,'" says Rondell. "Even seasoned pros get bruised and tattered [in a flying harness]. They get wire marks and they're rubbed raw. But, [I told him], 'Bear with me and I'll do the best I can to make you as comfortable as possible.'" Rondell drilled Routh in exercises to boost his core torso strength, needed whenever the scene required Routh to maintain an arms-out flying pose with only a few wires supporting his center of gravity. "I don't think [Routh] ever loved it, but he did a fantastic job with it."

The moment at the beginning of every Superman flight when the character leaves the ground was one of the trickiest beats to nail down. Does Superman slowly levitate, or shoot up like a bullet? At what point does his natural anti-gravity take over and cancel his body weight? Rondell insisted that Routh spend hours strapped into a simple up-and-down wire rig, practicing takeoffs and landings over and over again. "More than anything, it was for the timing,"

the effects
of superman returns

he explains. "I would establish a cadence, so [Routh] could prepare himself to know when the wires were coming on. A lot of times it was as subtle as [Routh] dropping his hips and presetting, then letting the wires raise him up. [That way] there wasn't a jerk, and it became one motion."

Rondell likened Superman's soaring to that of a fighter jet, yet he still wanted the character to hit the iconic positions that audiences expect from the Man of Steel. "We went through all the comic book poses," he says, giving special credit to *Superman Returns* movement coach Terry Notary. "[We looked] at beautiful lines, hand gestures, and how [Superman] initiates a turn by drawing an arm across, almost like a bodysurfer would carve across the face of a wave." For practice, Routh spent hours in a swimming pool, learning how the human body reacts to force and gravity.

Rondell also coordinated the fight scene between Superman and Lex Luthor, in which the Man of Steel takes the brunt of the pain. Rondell blocked out the action and taught Routh, a newcomer to film, how to "sell" a punch by throwing back his head. "Kevin Spacey [was already] very good at it," he notes. "Being a stage actor, he's done his share of hand-to-hand work."

Brandon Routh wasn't the only actor to enlist in Rondell's boot camp. Lois Lane enjoys her own trip to the sky, after a rooftop rendezvous inspires Superman to take her on a romantic airborne escape. Perhaps referring to a similar scene in 1978's *Superman: The Movie*, Rondell notes that his crew worked to make it appear that Lois is supported by Superman, as opposed to a "Peter Pan scenario" where she's flying alongside him. "[Here] she's actually draped on him slightly, so you get the feeling that he's doing the flying," he says. Rondell likened the sequence to a dance.

Stephan Bender plays the teenaged Clark Kent in flashback sequences set on the Smallville farm. The flashbacks show how young Clark first learned to leap tall buildings in a single bound, so Rondell trained the young actor to make prodigious jumps with the assistance of a wire rig. "He was fantastic," praises Rondell. "He'd never done a movie before, but he's a natural athlete, and he was so enthusiastic and so willing. He couldn't get enough. It made the first week or so of shooting really terrific."

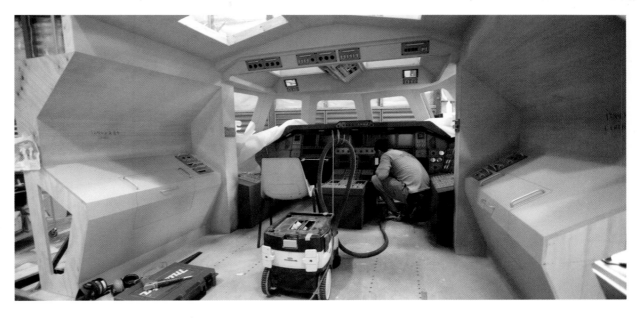

Enormous sound stages and great swathes of green screen allowed the filmmakers to tell their story with as much visual flair and precision as possible. The result is a film that captures all the dynamism and energy that would be expected of a Superman epic.

Time Inc. Home Entertainment
Publisher   Richard Fraiman
Executive Director, Marketing Services   Carol Pittard
Director, Retail & Special Sales   Tom Mifsud
Marketing Director, Branded Businesses   Swati Rao
Director, New Product Development   Peter Harper
Financial Director   Steven Sandonato
Assistant General Counsel   Dasha Smith Dwin
Prepress Manager   Emily Rabin
Book Production Manager   Jonathan Polsky
Product Manager   Victoria Alfonso
Associate Prepress Manager   Anne-Michelle Gallero

special *thanks*

Bryan Singer, Michael Dougherty, Dan Harris, Emma Rodgers
and Maureen Squillace at Warner Bros., the talented cast and
crew of *Superman Returns*, David James, Chris Cerasi,
Georg Brewer, Steve Korté, Barbara Rich, Bozena Bannett,
Alexandra Bliss, Glenn Buonocore, Suzanne Janso,
Robert Marasco, Brooke McGuire, Chavaughn Raines,
Ilene Schreider, Adriana Tierno, Britney Williams,
Jared K. Fletcher, Shawn Knapp, Henry Manfra,
Nick J. Napolitano, Scott Nybakken and Fred Ruiz.